THE Misadventures of Frederick

WRITTEN BY **BEN MANLEY**

ILLUSTRATED BY **EMMA CHICHESTER CLARK**

How to make a paper aeroplane

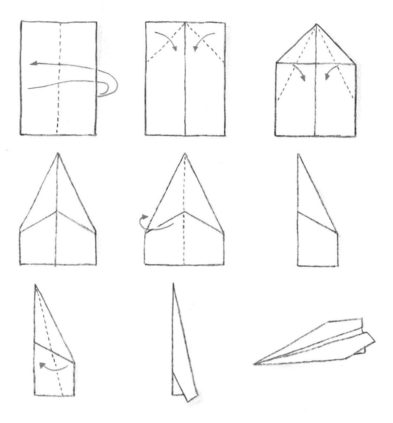

For Rajul ~ BM
For Francesca and Sam ~ ECC

First published 2019 by Two Hoots
This edition published 2020 by Two Hoots
an imprint of Pan Macmillan
The Smithson
6 Briset Street
London EC1M 5NR
Associated companies throughout the world
www.panmacmillan.com
ISBN:978-1-5098-5154-6
Text copyright © Ben Manley 2019
Illustrations copyright © Emma Chichester Clark 2019
Moral rights asserted.

1 3 5 7 9 8 6 4 2

A CIP catalogue record for this book is available from the British Library.
Printed in China
The illustrations in this book were created using watercolour.

www.twohootsbooks.com

Hello.
I can see you from the forest.

You look bored.

Would you like to go for an ice cream?

My favourite flavour is chocolate.

Love,
Emily x

FROM THE DESK OF
FREDERICK LEOPOLD NADELBAUM

My Dearest Emily,
The woodlark's melody floats
across the shimmering sky.

It is with bitter regret that
I inform you I may not
come out to eat ice creams
today, on account that I might
be sick into my music box.
Sorrowfully yours,
Frederick

FROM THE DESK OF
FREDERICK LEOPOLD NADELBAUM

My Dearest Emily,
The finches flutter in the sycamores, startling the drowsy dormouse.

It is with bitter regret that I inform you I may not come out to climb trees today on account that I might break both of my collar bones.

Sorrowfully yours,
Frederick

My Dearest Emily,

The wild rose rambles by the shady trail.

It is with bitter regret that I inform you I may not come out to ride bikes today on account that I might graze all the skin off my bottom.

Sorrowfully yours,
Frederick

FROM THE DESK OF
FREDERICK LEOPOLD NADELBAUM

My Dearest Emily,

The lonely salmon makes his ragged run upstream.

It is with bitter regret that I inform you I may not go swimming in the lake today on account that I might catch pneumonia and have to go to Switzerland.

Sorrowfully yours,
Frederick

Hi Frederick,
I'm exploring the forest today.
Please come.
Love Emily x

FROM THE DESK OF
FREDERICK LEOPOLD NADELBAUM

My Dearest Emily,
The melancholy wind sighs through the golden oak.

It is with bitter regret that I inform you I may not explore the forest today, on account that I might be remorselessly stung by hornets.

Sorrowfully yours,
Frederick

My Dearest Emily

The snow thaws on the bright mountain bringing forth the bluebell.

It is with great joy that I inform you my head has returned to its natural shape and I will be discharged from the sting clinic tomorrow.

Wanna get an ice cream?

Love,
Frederick x